Oddies®

This book
belongs to:

....

Oddies Limited, Maritime House, Grafton Square, London, SW4 0JW
www.oddieworld.com

Text copyright © Oddies Limited, 2004
Illustrations copyright © Oddies Limited, 2004

All rights reserved.

No part of this publication may be reproduced, translated into a machine
language, stored in a retrieval system, transmitted in any form or by any means,
lent, resold, hired out nor be otherwise circulated without the prior written
permission of the publisher, in any form of binding or cover other than that in
which it is published and without a similar condition being imposed on the
subsequent purchaser.

A CIP catalogue record for this book is available from the British Library.

First Published in Great Britain in 2004 by Oddies Limited.

ISBN 1-904745-17-2

Printed in Great Britain

Ballet Oddie

To Caitlin

Grant Slatter

The ballerina put her favourite pair of socks into the washing machine. She added some washing powder and shut the door.

"Chug-chug, whirr, chug-chug, whirr," went the washing machine. Then it did something strange.

It spun extra fast and all the bubbles bounced around wildly. The machine ballooned. Then there was a supersonic WHOOSH as one of the socks disappeared.

The sock was called Ballet Oddie and she was zooming through space towards Oddieworld. "Perhaps I'm going for a holiday to beautiful Oddieworld," she said.

Ballet Oddie floated down into Oddieworld and popped out of her bubble. She had landed on Bad Oddie Island! "Can you help me?" said a soft voice behind her.

It was Sock Fairy. "Princess Oddie needs rescuing," she said. "I can't stay here," said Ballet Oddie. "I'm a dainty dancer, not a rugged rescuer." Then she did a perfect pirouette.

Ballet Oddie stopped spinning and saw that Sock Fairy had disappeared. A ribbon had appeared in her place. "What a pretty gift!" she said. "Almost as pretty as me."

"Bad Oddie Island is not pretty though – so I'm not staying here," said Ballet Oddie. Then she set off to find a way to get to Good Oddie Island.

As she passed Toenail Woods she got a scary surprise.
She was about to cry when she realised no-one was
there to see her. "I'll save it up for later," she said.

Ballet Oddie wandered on unhappily.

She crossed a dirty river...

...went around the edge of a smelly bog...

BOOTLACE BOG

...and arrived at a beach.

Then Ballet Oddie heard something.
"Is anyone there?" she said. "I need help!"
"I need more help than you do," said a voice behind her.

It was Princess Oddie. "I was invited to a party here – but it was a Bad Oddie trick. Now my bubble power has nearly run out. Soon I'll sink down and then I'll never see my love again," she said.

Ballet Oddie wasn't going to be outshone by Princess Oddie.
"I will probably faint and fall in too," she said.
"Fear not, ladies," said a voice in the darkness. "Magical help is at hand!"

It was Wizzo. "I know a spell that makes things fly up."
"Oh yes!" said Princess Oddie. "Fly me out of here
so that I can see my love again."
"Ah yes...him!" said Wizzo.

This is gonna be good.

Then he whispered the magic words.
"*Flyinus Hoof Exland, come out of the sand.*"

There was a big bang and a puff of smoke then everyone flew up into the air. Everyone, that is, except Princess Oddie.

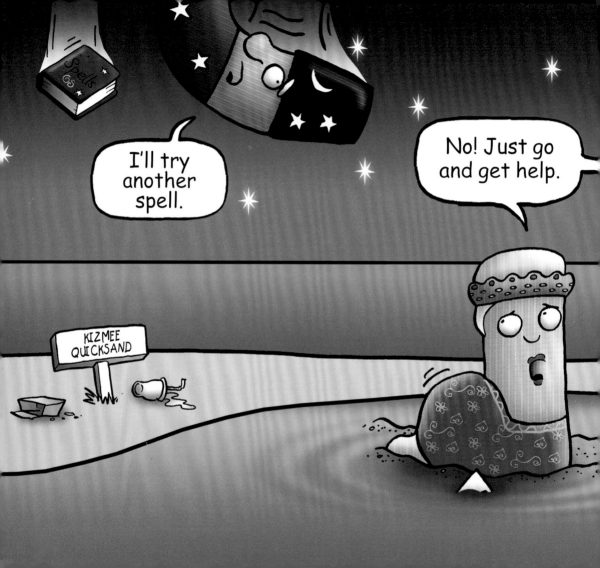

"Listen," said Ballet Oddie, "there's no point in making a *song and dance* about this now. Let's just sort it out ourselves."

"OK, what's the plan?" said Princess Oddie.
"We'll use my ribbon," said Ballet Oddie. "Just
wrap one end around you and hang on."

Ballet Oddie bounced on the branch
and then spun off.

Princess Oddie was pulled up and out of the quicksand.
Then they both let go of the ribbon.

"Thanks Ballet Oddie - you're amazing!" said Princess Oddie.
"That's true," said Ballet Oddie. "I always put the needs
of others before my own - it's just the way I am."

"Now I must be off," she added. "I need
to find my way to Good Oddie Island."
"I can take you both there," said a familiar voice.

It was Sock Fairy. "We'd love you to stay in Oddieworld forever," she said, "but I'll magic you back if that's what you'd really like."

"I'd like to stay – but only on Good Oddie Island where it's beautiful, just like me," said Ballet Oddie. "I could make up a lovely dance for you all."

The next evening in Oddietown, Ballet Oddie performed her dance. It was called Duck Lake.

Back home, the ballerina danced around looking
for her missing sock but she didn't find it.

She took a flying leap into bed
and then asked herself...

"Where do those odd socks go?"

Have you got the complete collection?

Ballet Oddie is the seventh book in the Oddies series. Read the stories of all the other Oddies and their adventures in Oddieworld.

The signposts on Good Oddie Island are all muddled up so Sock Fairy sends for **Police Oddie** - but he soon needs to call for help himself!

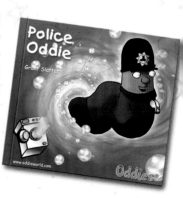

The secret is out, odd socks go to Oddieworld! Find out how Oddieworld was formed and how **Wizzo**, **Witchy** and **Sock Fairy** became stuck there.

Witchy is cooking up a storm in Oddieworld and Sock Fairy needs some help from **Footy Oddie** - but can he find a way to stop the rain?

Litterbug has a tummy ache and nobody knows why, so Sock Fairy sends for **Nurse Oddie** - but can she make this patient better in a tick?

Witchy wants the Oddie Crown Jewels and calls **Robber Oddie** to help her get them - but he soon learns that crime doesn't pay.

Every Oddie has a story to tell!

Take your child on an adventure...
...to Oddieworld!

Visit www.oddieworld.com and help your child gain basic computer skills and have fun at the same time.

Games • Puzzles • Colouring-in
Free Oddiecards • Competitions

Buy Oddies books & Matching Odd Socks™

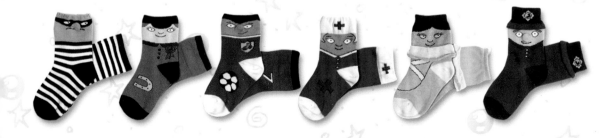

There are lots of games to play plus one secret game!

Find it and complete it and we'll send you a **FREE Oddies poster!**

www.**oddieworld**.com

Please Note: Use of this website may permanently IMPROVE your child's hand/eye co-ordination and intelligence!

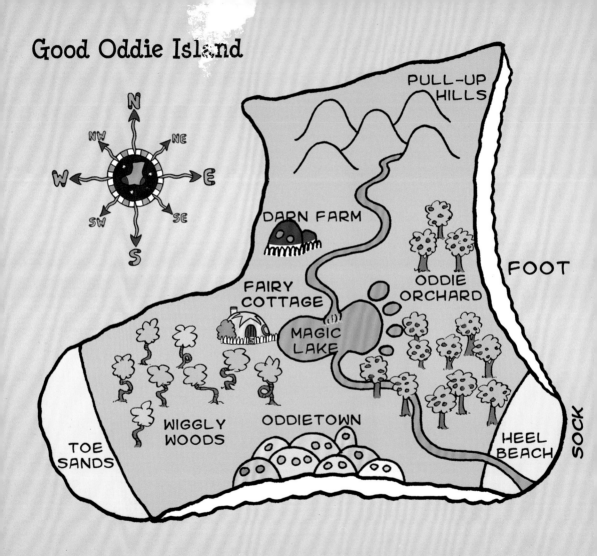